When Memories Catch Fire

By: Chad Smith

Every word in this book was written by me. No AI was used for ideas or editing.
This comes from the heart.

To find more books by me visit:

www.gattaca.world

Staten House

For Bryan Center. Brother, we are building the greatest playlist of all time.

Long after humanity is gone, if the aliens come and find the playlist...they will understand.

"Fire is never a gentle master."

– Proverb

"Last night I dreamed about you. What happened in detail I can hardly remember, all I know is that we kept merging into one another. I was you, you were me. Finally you somehow caught fire."

- Franz Kafka

Ardens umquam consistetne

Table of Contents

Forward

It was unfair for Chad to ask me to write this for him. I mean, it's totally fair for me, I love the guy. It's unfair for you because you're going to get a very biased opinion of the author of the words on these pages. So get ready for a sappy foreword full of gushing sentiment.

The line from Stephen King's "The Body" is true and I think about it daily; "I never had any friends later on in life like the ones I had when I was 12 — Jesus, did you?" It's hard to make friends in your 40s. To make a friend that becomes closer than family in this banana pudding ripe banana stage of life has to be even rarer. Finding someone you can share deep thoughts and feelings with free of judgement? Well that's god damned near impossible.

I knew of Chad for years as he married a friend from high school but we really connected while waiting for a Sebastian Bach concert to start. We discovered we loved a lot of the same stuff, even extending to a mutual high school paramour. Most importantly, we had a deep attraction to sadness. Not because of Sebastian Bach, he's still amazing. We just downright loved wallowing in sad books, movies, and especially music. There's something about finding an artist you've never met expressing themselves about things you have always felt but were unable to express that resonated with us. Writing that out makes me understand why we became close.
Sadness permeates a lot of life and while instinctively you want to avoid it, sometimes it feels good to sit with it. So sit with it here, there's a lot of it. I was honored to be able to read these before you and I have my favorites. Hopefully you find a piece in here that plucks the heart strings.

P.S. - I know somewhere Lori is happy we get to be in each other's lives...

-   Bryan Center, 2024

Burning in Estes Park

(For and written with...Andrew)

It exploded

out of the cold

and insects

and someone's cigarette

(whoever it was)

      (fuck you)

We choked

      and looked

at black and orange skies

      at noon

sitting in stopped traffic

Trying to get away

get out

breathing in the smoke
      choking

We smell the sun
      as fear pushes people

            away

burned up lives
            orange into black

while we race to get
        away.

Transcending

"Then Mary took about a pint of pure nard, an expensive perfume; she poured it on Jesus' feet and wiped his feet with her hair. And the house was filled with the fragrance of the perfume."

- John 12:3 - Bible

and here I lay at your feet

my tears fall

and no

      it isn't raining

but the water begins

to clean your feet

I can't inhale

     I seem
         only
            to be
               able
                  to exhale

could you save anyone

     even if you were still alive?

The child of a killer

I am just

the child of a killer

a killer of fun

of running through the house

of making noise

a killer of my father's affection

a murderer of tucking me in
at night

a killer of compassion

a killer who hand-fed
the squirrels in our front yard

a killer
a murderer

blood painted faces
and splatter on the walls

a murderer of hope

     a killer of futures

Cold Sheets

Sleeping in your red sheets
        always made me calm

I remember

        you would get up

at 3am

and open all the windows

the salt

        the sea

                the air

floated over our bodies

heaving in the night.

        Sometimes

                I wake up now

                        shivering.

The paper and wind

I had written something for you

    drawn you

        in simple shades of pencil

           grey

        on thick yellow paper.

I left my apartment
carrying it in my hand

I got on the subway at Woodhaven Blvd

    when I got off

        the subway wind carried you away.

as i turn to dust

it is hot in July
in Greenwood, South Carolina
walking up this dusty rock-filled road
I am looking for something shiny

I am small and alone
my mother is locked in the bedroom
of my grandmother's lake house
livid that we are here

My father is arguing with my grandfather
about some bible verse
and who is going to hell

My grandfather was kind
to me
even though he read the bible
cover to cover
year after year

He was afraid of cars
and hallways

He walked five miles a day
maybe that helped

He had a recurring dream
that he was walking down a hallway
that never ended

He wondered if that was hell.

When I was ten

A lady ran

A stop sign

And ran him over
breaking 38 bones in his body
he died within hours

I hope he is not walking down a hallway

somewhere.

Bedposts

I remember white bed posts

and your blonde hair

in my mouth

in my eyes

and on my face

as you slept

I could turn my head and see

A statue of a cat and a dog

in the window

against the winter moon

shining over our bodies.

enchantment
stripping away loneliness
with the withering leaves
falling down into buckets
of water and shame
brought on by your madness
staring into mirrors
as you look for the inside
of your soul
you find nothing

Dry humping for god

We had to pray
as a group

Sometimes
it would go on and on
and we were

required

to keep our eyes closed

This happened in most of our classes
in high school

One teacher
would hump the podium
in his classroom

while he was calling out to god.

Joints

We were at that concert
      Candlebox
           when the lead singer threw
               a handful

of joints into the crowd

Your blonde hair was so short
      it didn't have the right effect

When we got in the pit
      I could feel my long hair whipping
         against my face
           and yours

      I kissed you like we were going to die.

Lamp Posts Down Bleeker Street

I walk down these grey sidewalks
thinking about
my father
in pain and dying

a sudden gust of

      cool air

         hits me

as I walk under three in a row

they go

from shining

      into darkness

What is following me?

Those folders

For Susan

We were sitting in your mom's classroom
alone
and I don't remember why
I think we were hiding from chapel

I knocked a stack of folders
off her desk
and you helped me
stack them back up

I re-ordered them as I remembered
the colors and how they were stacked

You said something kind.

We went to see a Presidential candidate at the Chattanooga airport
we were in a thick crowd
and my anxiety disorder
that I kept secret
kicked

I ended up on the sidelines
leaning against an ugly grey concrete wall
gasping

I called you that night
and told you about my anxiety
and the meds

You said something kind.

We started the Breakfast Club.

we would meet
before school with Joe
and bitch about high school.
One day I was upset
about the screaming in my parents' house

You said something kind.

We graduated high school
I was ready for college
I had a shitty retail job
My girlfriend had dumped me
on our Senior Trip

We were with some friends
at a playground
sand everywhere
on a swing set
talking about our future

       lives

at 1am

I could not stop my sadness

You said something kind.

You look like you've seen a ghost

I was back in town
for some holiday

And I walked into a bar
and there you were
in a white dress

leaning on the bar
smiling
looking so at home

I couldn't breathe

I went to the bathroom
and gasped at the mirror

I broke into silver
I could not look back

Another time...Maybe the last

We were crossing
    the Mississippi line
        your wife screaming
            through your cell phone

we had been gone
    far too long

now older
    I see myself
sweating
    in that red car

and that was
    our last time

I should have
    told you
how much
    you meant to me

when I could.

But there we were

    there we were.

Walking Back

It was Manhattan
in early winter

I was at some conference
that would end early every day

I would wander through the streets
orange leaves blowing across my feet

the air would whipper through my hair
I would stuff my hands in my coat
and smile

taking the long way back to my hotel
I would just wander

feeling the vibrations of the city

One day I went in a random Irish bar
Heatmiser was playing over
the speaker in the corner

Sometimes it's better being alone

I looked at myself
through the bottles
at the bar mirror

Out on the street

     snowflakes hit me on the cheek.

                   lie

and you're lying, sad girl
forgetting rumbling days
inside my stomach,
all these acids eating away
at you
eating away the girl I love

those tattoos you adorn
on your soft skin – silent
glaring at me, mocking you
and you're lying sad girl
lying to those empty skies

and tell me of your dreams
of our fair-haired children
who break our hearts
with their fragile wanderings

your open eyes tell me of happiness
but you're lying to a sad girl
and a lonely, frightened boy.

Forgiveness

"There is no such thing as forgiveness. People just have short memories."

"Haunted Houses." True Detective, created by Nic Pizzolatto, Season 1, Episode 6, Home Box Office, Inc., 2014.

Religiousness
    tells us to forgive

    to turn the other cheek

    to do unto others

who were these people
and where have they gone?

did you think it mattered?

the 400-pound baptist preacher
sweating
and roaring
from the pulpit

Tithe   or burn   in hell

The priest talking
his little altar boy
into the back
      feet like ash

The leaders

crucifying the poor to the cross

I thought vengeance belonged to the lord

He must be asleep

these precious blue bluffs
we sing to each other
swimming through this murk
did you ever see?
and I know what you're saying?
shaking your body on the dance floor
wish yourself away
out of this life
I could give it all to you.

The death of Jerome Morrow

"You lent me your dream."

-    Jerome Morrow

"Gattaca." Directed by Andrew Niccol, Performances by Ethan Hawke,
Uma Thurman Jude Law,
Columbia Pictures, 1997.

you finally got it right

in traffic the first time

        you paralyzed yourself

now as you climb into

        the furnace

                and hold your silver medal

what were you thinking

        when you flipped the switch

and set yourself

        ablaze

                you were never second best.

Under the sky

"Pretty thing," she called it,
        wandering around in her private forest
        thick, green trees covered
                an empty blue sky, offering hope

The dirt trails ran in circles
        I never
                could find my way out

though I often had dreams
        of reaching the edge and seeing

you waiting for me,
as I lay in the cool dirt at night
        looking for the silver moon
                through the leaves

I looked for you in the summer
        during the thunder and the rain
                water pouring from my face
                and I felt the darkness
                        of your darkness.

You were always running
        lost

            hope
                far from your sight

Blue Phone Booth

I've stood here with you
feeling your warmth beside me
against this cold wind,
looking out across the ocean

Now I feel as if I'm sinking
in the rising blue waves

I raise my eyes at the sight
of the orange moon sliding from
behind a purple cloud

I want to see you run
through barren fields again,
the way I remember

straight into my arms

At the carnival,
we ran from that half-drunk clown
and I stole cotton candy while you
distracted the fifteen-year-old kid
with your winking eyes and wavering lips,

remember?

But now I cross the street
where the blue phone booth used to be
and call you on my iPhone
just to let you hear me hang up

one more time.

and you say

that love has no ending
these words send shivers
down spines of young girls
and careless lovers
but these thick words
mean a lot of nothing

playing the fool

I.
the machines play on,
orchestrating our movements,
pulling our invisible strings
as we walk through the city streets
in the sweeping dusk.
the whir of the gears
ring in our hero's ears
as he climbs his glass tower
to survey the landscape
of his misery.
the machines pull stretches
on our hero's face
as his plastic eyes look
out over the city,
wanting desperately to find
the wavering pink lights
of the machine's underbelly
as his princess may be there.

But the gears turn
the machines groan,
the ground trembles and our hero's
glass tower shakes.
The people below look up in wonder
as if the gods in heaven are angry
with them.
And we wonder if tonight
we will sleep soundly,
if the moon will shine its golden rays
onto every sleeping child.

Meanwhile, the princess sleeps
near the machines' warm engines,

dreaming the dreams, the machines
build for her...(to be continued)

You (again)

Won't touch me
cold again

off in a world

of some sort
I can't comprehend
or enter

maybe the planes fly upside down
maybe the sidewalks are made of glass
maybe people protest with signs saying "No LOVE"

I can't sleep
the skies are black
I see no stars

I pull another blanket onto me
even though it is warm

     and shiver

Panic in the Wrong Place at the Wrong Time

Raoul Duke:
"Panic. It crept up my spine like the first rising vibes of an acid frenzy."

- Thompson, Hunter S. Fear and Loathing in Las Vegas: A Savage Journey to the Heart of the American Dream. Random House, 1971.

I can't breathe.

cold sweat pops up through my skin

    all over

my lower body vibrates

    my foot seizes and cramps

I shake

I can't breathe.

my heart races

I can't speak

try to slow it down

    try to slow it down

        try to slow it down

panting

    I start to cry

I can't breathe.

Rainbows and Glitter

My son's sixth birthday

He wanted a piñata

We made a unicorn
pink and blue and white
fluffy
with strings

we filled it with candy

      and glitter

the boys and girls

beat it with bats

I thought I heard it crying

      and it finally broke

I felt something break in me

the glitter flew through the air

      onto their smiling faces

            eyes open in the air

And did you wonder

I went to a wedding the other day
and everyone was dressed in white
and it was like ours
did we see that many smiles?

it seems so ridiculous
two people, arms intertwined
pour gold champagne into one another's mouth
and believe in their darkest depths,
that this will be forever

forever like us.

but in the end
things are the same
(for all of us)
the cold walls rise up
and you cannot walk through them
and you cannot talk through them

and had you known
that we would hurl such bitter glass words
deep at each other's heart

would you have looked at me the same way
when you held that glass to my lips?

When the Swingset was the universe

dangling from those chains
suspended in the air
I could fly into the honey autumn air
as a bird or winged animal
I was the freest creature alive.

Years later, I sat in that little seat
and lifted off the ground again,
imagining I was a pilot
sailing toward the clouds.

The October sky was bright and blue
endless and weightless with the memory
of infinite trips I took in my mind.
I wanted another journey.

The wind was cool and sweet,
I could almost feel...
the leaves drifted in rainbows
toward the ground.

memory (for Joe)

it was a memory that some
eyeless blonde kicked up
I had forgotten my glasses that day
and all the signs pointed away
I couldn't start crying
but the tears flowed,
and though I wanted to build
a wall bigger than Pink
ever could have dreamt of,
but I couldn't stop the flood
of childhood rushing over me.

I remember the day you drew
a circle in the dirt and wrote
"pals" in the middle.
The circle shall not be broken,
you said,
but you broke it with such violence
I still cannot speak of it.
Jon said, "gotta hold on to what we've got,"
but sometimes all the faces
blur and I can't see any further
than I can reach out
with these trembling hands.

The cold white tile II

On the hospital floor again
       hard
              I push my cheek
                     on the lines between
                           the tiles

and feel the cold
        I wonder if who has died in this spot

outside my room

a man is screaming for a blanket
      "I'm cold! I'm cold!"

my half-closed lids
gaze out across the floor

to the door closed

I

     shiver
          tremble
               to smile

as I fall into a dreamless sleep

but then the dream again

a shiny black night
       driving up a grey gravel driveway
I am the passenger
       the house is bathed in blue lights

           and dark iron gates hover

before

     me

and the floor again
       someone is speaking

The nurse who loves me
rubs my shoulders
I crawl to my knees and she helps me
back into bed.

She injects something into my IV

and I fall

     fall

          fall

ice and dark

and finally I remembered

"You are at once both the quiet and the confusion of my heart."

-    Franz Kafka

we were at a theme park

Six Flags

      over Georgia

looking in this grey rearview mirror

you broke my heart that day

into so many sharp stars

they still cut my feet   when I walk

over them

you had a boyfriend that you liked to talk about

but on that day

you only

      had smiles

        for me

and getting on the river ride

with our friends

you clung to me

like the world was going to end

the ride ended

you walked away

and I thought I had lost it all

maybe now I just remembered

Ambien Nights

When they work

it's

blue

ink

down

and

icy

drives

and I go into the deep

and other times

I see armies

and navies

of words

battle

all for nothing.

The barn

It comes in furies

    rips

        roars

            in wild anger

and I want

    to burn

that blue barn at the edge of the road

I just want to see it

the place where I found you

in red fire

    at night

smoke billowing into

a starless sky

the full moon

hanging on

    at the edge.

Go back

For Andrew and John

and up the driveway
and look for the shadow
of your dad's orange VW.
Can you still hear the basketball bouncing
from those many summer nights?
Walk across the road
and into the forest,
find the place where you read Tolkien
and turned the woods around you
into Middle Earth.
Walk down to the gravel pit,
can you still hear your BB Gun
pinging off the aluminum cans?

When you leave, this will all disappear,
swallowed up by progress and truck stops,
but right now

      it lives in your mind.

Walk down the road,
into the house, and your old room,
and lie on the bed,
look at the NFL posters on the wall.

This was your childhood.

Once a country

It was storming in Cuba
as our ship came in
grey
      grey
          grey

the waves crashing over
      the concrete dock walls

smashing
      the spray spiraling
          into the air

walking down the streets
      then the bright blue cars
          built from scraps
             of 1960's GM, Ford, and Chryslers

carried us on the hunt for cigars

our host was full of smiles
      and stories

of a land without shower heads or toilet paper

again on the streets
      we walk

the smell of sewage
      in our eyes

we pass Penelope Cruz
      her smile

not enough for a Havana night

out of my mouth
the smoke from a Cohiba

Trains

jagged

    the lightning

        thunders into the ground

purple and white skies

the china trembles

in the distance the

    sound of a

        roar

           of a train

the lights go out

    the tornado decides

    what to touch

Kat

the last time we talked
I was writing so much

but you said you couldn't
anymore

you were afraid it was your meds
and so was I

in Cedar Key
we discovered that old book store

I bought *Edisto* by Padgett Powell
and you bought a book of poetry

we talked about moving there
with future lovers

then we drank red wine
read our books
and fell asleep

The Peace Letters

come in brown envelopes

    I'm always afraid to open them

      I'm always afraid

Your curled lettering with the
    lipstick kisses

speaking of things we did long ago
    and things we might do
        one day

so many years ago
    salt and sand between our toes
      the salt cold water
        the smell of seaweed
          rotting on the shore

we were out on our boards
    waiting for sunrise
      and the next good set

sharks bumping up against our legs

even then
    you wouldn't let us go in

      you were looking for the dark.

When I was that way...back when

At the end of the cul-de-sac
     that red brick house

with the two lower windows
     smashed in
         some bricks
have fallen off
     into the yard of weeds

push open the unlocked door

the staircase has fallen
     there is no way to get downstairs

     anymore

       you hear someone still breathing

we tremble

once
long ago
I would wake up alone
and you would be

across the bedroom
on the wall
slumped in fear
eyes wide

I would speak
and wrap my arms
around you
and we would go back to bed

Now we lie
asleep in the dark
my arms wrapped
around you
under your breasts

you cry

we tremble

if only
      I could calm you

          again

That Open Door

at the end of the hallway

walls green

1989

a home for people
          who couldn't deal with

                    others

I had to stay
          for 30 days

my roommates came and
          went

so many cutters
          so many scars

a variety of orange and white pills

in a world without
          shoes or shoelaces
                    or TV

only puzzles of countryside views
          green and blue and red and white

no showering
          without a nurse watching

standing in the shower room
          I would watch

the water fall
      splash
on my ankes
      into the silver drain

one night
      the door ajar
            unlocked

I think I saw
      yellow petals on the floor

As I neared the end I saw the white line in the red clay track

as I fell...

the chalk breathing into my neck

,

Epilogue

"The fire you kindle for your enemy often burns yourself more than them."

- Chinese Proverb

"I had so much fire in me and so many plans."

- Claude Monet

Acknowledgments

This book would not have happened without the encouragement of my wife Amiee and my TIRELESS early readers and editors Bryan Center and Andrew Virdin. I love all of you.

Cover art by Andrew Virdin

About the Author

Chad Smith is a consultant and author hiding out in the Caribbean.